MAD LIBS®

EASTER EGGSTRAVAGANZA MAD LIBS

MAD LIBS
An Imprint of Penguin Random House LLC, New York

Mad Libs format and text copyright © 2013 by Penguin Random House LLC.
All rights reserved.

Concept created by Roger Price & Leonard Stern

Published by Mad Libs,
an imprint of Penguin Random House LLC, New York.
Printed in the USA.

Visit us online at www.penguinrandomhouse.com.

ISBN 9780843172522
16

MAD LIBS
INSTRUCTIONS

MAD LIBS® is a game for people who don't like games! It can be played by one, two, three, four, or forty.

● RIDICULOUSLY SIMPLE DIRECTIONS

In this tablet you will find stories containing blank spaces where words are left out. One player, the READER, selects one of these stories. The READER does not tell anyone what the story is about. Instead, he/she asks the other players, the WRITERS, to give him/her words. These words are used to fill in the blank spaces in the story.

● TO PLAY

The READER asks each WRITER in turn to call out a word—an adjective or a noun or whatever the space calls for—and uses them to fill in the blank spaces in the story. The result is a MAD LIBS® game.

When the READER then reads the completed MAD LIBS® game to the other players, they will discover that they have written a story that is fantastic, screamingly funny, shocking, silly, crazy, or just plain dumb—depending upon which words each WRITER called out.

● EXAMPLE (*Before* and *After*)

" _____ !" he said _____
　　　　　　EXCLAMATION　　　　　　　　　　　　　　　　ADVERB

as he jumped into his convertible _____ and
　　　　　　　　　　　　　　　　　　　　　　NOUN

drove off with his _____ wife.
　　　　　　　　　　ADJECTIVE

" _____*Ouch*_____ !" he said _____*stupidly*_____
　　　　EXCLAMATION　　　　　　　　　　　　　ADVERB

as he jumped into his convertible _____*cat*_____ and
　　　　　　　　　　　　　　　　　　　　NOUN

drove off with his _____*brave*_____ wife.
　　　　　　　　　　ADJECTIVE

QUICK REVIEW

In case you have forgotten what adjectives, adverbs, nouns, and verbs are, here is a quick review:

An ADJECTIVE describes something or somebody. *Lumpy, soft, ugly, messy,* and *short* are adjectives.

An ADVERB tells how something is done. It modifies a verb and usually ends in "ly." *Modestly, stupidly, greedily,* and *carefully* are adverbs.

A NOUN is the name of a person, place, or thing. *Sidewalk, umbrella, bridle, bathtub,* and *nose* are nouns.

A VERB is an action word. *Run, pitch, jump,* and *swim* are verbs. Put the verbs in past tense if the directions say PAST TENSE. *Ran, pitched, jumped,* and *swam* are verbs in the past tense.

When we ask for A PLACE, we mean any sort of place: a country or city (*Spain, Cleveland*) or a room (*bathroom, kitchen*).

An EXCLAMATION or SILLY WORD is any sort of funny sound, gasp, grunt, or outcry, like *Wow!, Ouch!, Whomp!, Ick!,* and *Gadzooks!*

When we ask for specific words, like a NUMBER, a COLOR, an ANIMAL, or a PART OF THE BODY, we mean a word that is one of those things, like *seven, blue, horse,* or *head.*

When we ask for a PLURAL, it means more than one. For example, *cat* pluralized is *cats.*

MAD LIBS® is fun to play with friends, but you can also play it by yourself! To begin with, DO NOT look at the story on the page below. Fill in the blanks on this page with the words called for. Then, using the words you have selected, fill in the blank spaces in the story.

Now you've created your own hilarious MAD LIBS® game!

WHO IS THE
REAL EASTER BUNNY?

ADJECTIVE _____

ADJECTIVE _____

NOUN _____

PLURAL NOUN _____

NOUN _____

PLURAL NOUN _____

ADJECTIVE _____

PLURAL NOUN _____

PLURAL NOUN _____

VERB _____

NOUN _____

VERB _____

ADJECTIVE _____

PLURAL NOUN _____

NOUN _____

A PLACE _____

MAD LIBS®
WHO IS THE
REAL EASTER BUNNY?

How much do you *really* know about the _____ Easter Bunny?
ADJECTIVE

Here's the _____ scoop on this mysterious _____ .
ADJECTIVE   NOUN

Q: Does the Easter Bunny have magical _____ ?
PLURAL NOUN

A: Absolutely. How else could one furry _____ deliver candy-
NOUN

filled _____ to children everywhere in one _____ night?
PLURAL NOUN   ADJECTIVE

Q: Santa has elves and reindeer to help him make and deliver

_____ on Christmas. Does the Easter Bunny have any right-
PLURAL NOUN

hand _____ ?
PLURAL NOUN

A: As far as we know, the Easter Bunny likes to _____ alone.
VERB

Like other bunnies, he is a very shy _____ and prefers to
NOUN

_____ all by himself.
VERB

Q: Where does the Easter Bunny live?

A: Only the Easter Bunny knows the answer to this _____
ADJECTIVE

question, though some _____ believe he lives in a cozy
PLURAL NOUN

_____ in (the) _____ .
NOUN   A PLACE

MAD LIBS® is fun to play with friends, but you can also play it by yourself! To begin with, DO NOT look at the story on the page below. Fill in the blanks on this page with the words called for. Then, using the words you have selected, fill in the blank spaces in the story.

Now you've created your own hilarious MAD LIBS® game!

HISTORY OF THE JELLY BEAN

ADJECTIVE _____

PLURAL NOUN _____

PART OF THE BODY (PLURAL) _____

NOUN _____

PLURAL NOUN _____

NUMBER _____

PART OF THE BODY (PLURAL) _____

PART OF THE BODY (PLURAL) _____

ADJECTIVE _____

NOUN _____

PLURAL NOUN _____

NOUN _____

ADJECTIVE _____

ADJECTIVE _____

MAD LIBS
HISTORY OF THE JELLY BEAN

Jelly beans aren't just Easter candy—they have a very long and

_____ history in the United _____ of America, dating
ADJECTIVE   PLURAL NOUN

all the way back to the 1800s. During the Civil War, Americans sent

jelly beans to soldiers to put smiles on their _____.
                                                PART OF THE BODY (PLURAL)

In the early 1900s, "penny candy"—sweets you could buy for just one

_____—became all the rage, and jelly _____ became
NOUN   PLURAL NOUN

more popular than ever. In the 1940s, during World War _____,
                                                          NUMBER

a chocolate shortage led people to turn to jelly beans to satisfy their

sweet _____. By the 1960s, even rock stars were
      PART OF THE BODY (PLURAL)

falling head over _____ for the _____ jelly
                  PART OF THE BODY (PLURAL)   ADJECTIVE

bean. When fans of the famous musical _____ the Beatles heard
                                        NOUN

the band liked the candy, they tossed _____ onto the stage at
                                        PLURAL NOUN

their concerts. In the 1980s, President Reagan said he needed a/an

_____ full of jelly beans just to get through _____
NOUN   ADJECTIVE

meetings. Some might say the United States itself is run on delicious,

_____ jelly beans!
ADJECTIVE

MAD LIBS® is fun to play with friends, but you can also play it by yourself! To begin with, DO NOT look at the story on the page below. Fill in the blanks on this page with the words called for. Then, using the words you have selected, fill in the blank spaces in the story.

Now you've created your own hilarious MAD LIBS® game!

A ROCKIN' EASTER EGG ROLL

PERSON IN ROOM _____

NOUN _____

PERSON IN ROOM _____

COLOR _____

VERB _____

CELEBRITY _____

CELEBRITY _____

PERSON IN ROOM _____

NOUN _____

ADJECTIVE _____

PLURAL NOUN _____

ADJECTIVE _____

ADJECTIVE _____

NOUN _____

NOUN _____

NOUN _____

PLURAL NOUN _____

NOUN _____

MAD LIBS

A ROCKIN' EASTER EGG ROLL

President _____ and the First _____,
PERSON IN ROOM   NOUN

_____, cordially invite you to the Easter Egg
PERSON IN ROOM

Roll at the _____ House in Washington, DC! This year's
COLOR

theme is "Rock and _____," and will have guests such as
VERB

_____, _____, and _____.
CELEBRITY   CELEBRITY   PERSON IN ROOM

The band One _____ will also be on hand to perform
NOUN

their number one hit, "What Makes You _____." In
ADJECTIVE

addition, there will be _____ to eat, _____ games
PLURAL NOUN   ADJECTIVE

to play, and of course, the _____ Easter Egg Roll itself,
ADJECTIVE

where each _____ will push a/an _____ through the
NOUN   NOUN

grass using a long-handled _____. It's guaranteed to be
NOUN

more fun than a barrel of _____! We hope to see you and
PLURAL NOUN

your _____ there!
NOUN

MAD LIBS® is fun to play with friends, but you can also play it by yourself! To begin with, DO NOT look at the story on the page below. Fill in the blanks on this page with the words called for. Then, using the words you have selected, fill in the blank spaces in the story.

Now you've created your own hilarious MAD LIBS® game!

SPOTTED: THE EASTER BUNNY

A PLACE _____

PART OF THE BODY _____

PERSON IN ROOM _____

ADJECTIVE _____

PART OF THE BODY _____

PLURAL NOUN _____

PLURAL NOUN _____

ADJECTIVE _____

PART OF THE BODY (PLURAL) _____

PERSON IN ROOM _____

NOUN _____

ADJECTIVE _____

SILLY WORD _____

PLURAL NOUN _____

PLURAL NOUN _____

MAD LIBS®
SPOTTED:
THE EASTER BUNNY

Attention, Channel 5 viewers! This just in. We have breaking news

from (the) _____, where the Easter Bunny has allegedly

A PLACE

been spotted! _____-witnesses at _____'s Grocery

PART OF THE BODY · PERSON IN ROOM

say the Easter Bunny was dressed incognito in dark sunglasses and

a/an _____ wig on his _____. He was reportedly

ADJECTIVE · PART OF THE BODY

shopping for plastic grass and jelly _____—perhaps to fill

PLURAL NOUN

little boys' and girls' Easter _____ this coming Easter

PLURAL NOUN

Sunday? But shoppers who spotted the Easter Bunny couldn't get a/an

_____ answer out of him: "When I saw him, I couldn't

ADJECTIVE

believe my own two _____," said _____.

PART OF THE BODY (PLURAL) · PERSON IN ROOM

"I said, 'Are you the Easter _____?' 'I guess I need a more

NOUN

_____ disguise!' he said, and he hopped off faster than you

ADJECTIVE

can say '_____'!" Well, there you have it, _____!

SILLY WORD · PLURAL NOUN

The Easter Bunny shops for his own _____, just like you!

PLURAL NOUN

MAD LIBS® is fun to play with friends, but you can also play it by yourself! To begin with, DO NOT look at the story on the page below. Fill in the blanks on this page with the words called for. Then, using the words you have selected, fill in the blank spaces in the story.

Now you've created your own hilarious MAD LIBS® game!

EASTER JOKES, PART 1

ADJECTIVE _____

ADJECTIVE _____

NOUN _____

ADJECTIVE _____

ADJECTIVE _____

PART OF THE BODY _____

NUMBER _____

ADJECTIVE _____

PART OF THE BODY _____

NOUN _____

ADJECTIVE _____

MAD LIBS®
EASTER JOKES, PART 1

Q: Why shouldn't you tell a/an _____ joke to a/an
<u>ADJECTIVE</u>

_____ egg?
<u>ADJECTIVE</u>

A: You might make the poor _____ crack up!
<u>NOUN</u>

Q: Why are you stuffing your mouth full of _____
<u>ADJECTIVE</u>

Easter candy?

A: Because it doesn't taste _____ if I stuff it in my
<u>ADJECTIVE</u>

_____!
<u>PART OF THE BODY</u>

Q: Is it true that eating _____ carrots a day gives you
<u>NUMBER</u>

_____ eyesight?
<u>ADJECTIVE</u>

A: Well, I've never seen a bunny wearing prescription glasses on his

_____, have you?
<u>PART OF THE BODY</u>

Q: Why did the Easter egg hide under a/an _____?
<u>NOUN</u>

A: He was just a/an _____ little chicken!
<u>ADJECTIVE</u>

MAD LIBS® is fun to play with friends, but you can also play it by yourself! To begin with, DO NOT look at the story on the page below. Fill in the blanks on this page with the words called for. Then, using the words you have selected, fill in the blank spaces in the story.

Now you've created your own hilarious MAD LIBS® game!

EASTER JOKES, PART 2

PLURAL NOUN _____

NOUN _____

PLURAL NOUN _____

NOUN _____

Knock, knock.

Who's there?

Some bunny.

Some bunny who?

Some bunny's been eating all my Easter _____!
PLURAL NOUN

Knock, knock.

Who's there?

Boo.

Boo who?

Don't cry! The Easter _____ will bring you more
NOUN

_____ next year!
PLURAL NOUN

Knock, knock.

Who's there?

Esther.

Esther who?

Esther Bunny, you silly _____!
NOUN

MAD LIBS® is fun to play with friends, but you can also play it by yourself! To begin with, DO NOT look at the story on the page below. Fill in the blanks on this page with the words called for. Then, using the words you have selected, fill in the blank spaces in the story.

Now you've created your own hilarious MAD LIBS® game!

BUNNY IN OUTER SPACE

NOUN _____

ADJECTIVE _____

PLURAL NOUN _____

VERB (PAST TENSE) _____

A PLACE _____

NOUN _____

PERSON IN ROOM _____

PERSON IN ROOM _____

PLURAL NOUN _____

ADJECTIVE _____

ADVERB _____

CELEBRITY _____

A PLACE _____

PART OF THE BODY _____

ADJECTIVE _____

PLURAL NOUN _____

NOUN _____

MAD LIBS
BUNNY IN OUTER SPACE

What's that in the sky? Is it a bird? Is it a/an _____? No! It's
                                                    NOUN

a/an _____ bunny rabbit! Chimpanzees, dogs, and
         ADJECTIVE

_____ have all made trips to outer space. But did you know
  PLURAL NOUN

that a rabbit _____ through space, too? Back in 1959,
                VERB (PAST TENSE)

(the) _____ sent a rabbit named Marfusha into outer space.
         A PLACE

When the rocket _____ took off, Marfusha had two dogs
                     NOUN

named _____ and _____ by her side. The three
        PERSON IN ROOM   PERSON IN ROOM

intrepid _____ had a/an _____ mission and made
           PLURAL NOUN   ADJECTIVE

it home _____, and Marfusha became more famous than
          ADVERB

_____. (The) _____ even issued a postage stamp
   CELEBRITY   A PLACE

with her _____ on it! After her _____ space
           PART OF THE BODY   ADJECTIVE

mission, Marfusha retired from the space program, eating as many

_____ as she pleased and dreaming of outer _____.
  PLURAL NOUN   NOUN

MAD LIBS® is fun to play with friends, but you can also play it by yourself! To begin with, DO NOT look at the story on the page below. Fill in the blanks on this page with the words called for. Then, using the words you have selected, fill in the blank spaces in the story.

Now you've created your own hilarious MAD LIBS® game!

EASTER AROUND THE WORLD

PLURAL NOUN _____

PLURAL NOUN _____

PLURAL NOUN _____

ADJECTIVE _____

PLURAL NOUN _____

NOUN _____

PART OF THE BODY _____

ADJECTIVE _____

PLURAL NOUN _____

PLURAL NOUN _____

NOUN _____

ADVERB _____

PLURAL NOUN _____

SILLY WORD _____

NOUN _____

A PLACE _____

MAD LIBS®
EASTER AROUND THE WORLD

In the United States, people usually celebrate Easter by decorating

_____ and hunting for Easter _____. But how do
<u>PLURAL NOUN</u>   <u>PLURAL NOUN</u>

_____ in other countries celebrate this _____ day?
<u>PLURAL NOUN</u>   <u>ADJECTIVE</u>

Australia: Instead of the Easter Bunny, the Easter Bilby visits little

girls and _____. A bilby is an endangered Australian
<u>PLURAL NOUN</u>

_____ with a long _____ and _____,
<u>NOUN</u>   <u>PART OF THE BODY</u>   <u>ADJECTIVE</u>

rabbitlike ears.

Germany: Here, _____ paint eggs just like we do in the
<u>PLURAL NOUN</u>

United States—but Germans hang them from _____
<u>PLURAL NOUN</u>

as decorations.

Poland: For the traditional Easter meal, butter is molded into the

shape of a/an _____ and eaten _____.
<u>NOUN</u>   <u>ADVERB</u>

Croatia: Families fill a basket with decorated eggs, ham, bread, and a

cake made from _____ called a/an _____. Then
<u>PLURAL NOUN</u>   <u>SILLY WORD</u>

they cover the basket with a/an _____ and take it to (the)
<u>NOUN</u>

_____.
<u>A PLACE</u>

MAD LIBS® is fun to play with friends, but you can also play it by yourself! To begin with, DO NOT look at the story on the page below. Fill in the blanks on this page with the words called for. Then, using the words you have selected, fill in the blank spaces in the story.

Now you've created your own hilarious MAD LIBS® game!

EASTER BASKET BONANZA

PART OF THE BODY _____

NOUN _____

NOUN _____

VERB (PAST TENSE) _____

NOUN _____

PLURAL NOUN _____

PLURAL NOUN _____

PLURAL NOUN _____

PLURAL NOUN _____

NOUN _____

PART OF THE BODY _____

PART OF THE BODY _____

EXCLAMATION _____

NOUN _____

NOUN _____

On Easter morning, I awoke with a twinkle in my _____.
                                                  PART OF THE BODY

Where did the Easter _____ hide my basket this year? I
                           NOUN

went searching and found mine tucked behind a/an _____.
                                                       NOUN

After discovering it, I _____ for joy. It was the biggest
                         VERB (PAST TENSE)

Easter _____ I'd ever seen, and it was spilling over with candy,
            NOUN

toys, and _____. There were candied _____,
            PLURAL NOUN   PLURAL NOUN

chocolate-covered _____, and plastic eggs filled with
                       PLURAL NOUN

_____. There was even a giant chocolate Easter
   PLURAL NOUN

_____! My favorite. I immediately pulled off the colored
      NOUN

foil wrapping and bit off its _____. Yummy! But
                                PART OF THE BODY

what I saw next in that Easter basket made my eyes pop out of my

_____. "_____!" I exclaimed. "The Easter
   PART OF THE BODY   EXCLAMATION

Bunny brought me the new _____ Recon video game!" This
                                NOUN

was the best Easter in the history of the _____!
                                                NOUN

MAD LIBS® is fun to play with friends, but you can also play it by yourself! To begin with, DO NOT look at the story on the page below. Fill in the blanks on this page with the words called for. Then, using the words you have selected, fill in the blank spaces in the story.

Now you've created your own hilarious MAD LIBS® game!

RABBIT SHOW JUMPING

PLURAL NOUN _____

A PLACE _____

VERB _____

A PLACE _____

VERB _____

ADJECTIVE _____

PLURAL NOUN _____

PLURAL NOUN _____

ADJECTIVE _____

PLURAL NOUN _____

NOUN _____

VERB _____

PART OF THE BODY (PLURAL) _____

NOUN _____

SAME NOUN _____

MAD LIBS®
RABBIT SHOW JUMPING

You've heard of horse show jumping, where horses and their riders

jump over tall _____. But what about rabbit show jumping?
_____PLURAL NOUN_____

The sport started in (the) _____ in the 1980s when children
_____A PLACE_____

began training rabbits to _____ in their own backyards.
_____VERB_____

Now, the sport is very popular in (the) _____, and it's
_____A PLACE_____

gaining popularity in the United States, too! But how do you get a

rabbit to _____ on command? Rabbits are naturally
_____VERB_____

_____ jumpers, so their handlers slowly train them to jump
___ADJECTIVE___

over larger and larger _____, rewarding them with carrots or
_____PLURAL NOUN_____

_____ when they do a/an _____ job. In
___PLURAL NOUN___   ___ADJECTIVE___

competition, the rabbits are scored on how many _____
_____PLURAL NOUN_____

they can clear without knocking over a/an _____, and on how
_____NOUN_____

quickly they can _____ through the obstacle course. Show
_____VERB_____

jumping gives rabbits much-needed exercise, which is good for their

hearts and _____. As they say, a healthy
___PART OF THE BODY (PLURAL)___

_____ is a happy _____!
___NOUN___   ___SAME NOUN___

MAD LIBS® is fun to play with friends, but you can also play it by yourself! To begin with, DO NOT look at the story on the page below. Fill in the blanks on this page with the words called for. Then, using the words you have selected, fill in the blank spaces in the story.

Now you've created your own hilarious MAD LIBS® game!

EGGHEAD
EGG-HUNT SKILLS

ADJECTIVE _____

PLURAL NOUN _____

NOUN _____

NOUN _____

NOUN _____

ADJECTIVE _____

NOUN _____

VERB (PAST TENSE) _____

PLURAL NOUN _____

VERB _____

PLURAL NOUN _____

PART OF THE BODY _____

PERSON IN ROOM _____

VERB _____

PLURAL NOUN _____

MAD☺LIBS®
EGGHEAD
EGG-HUNT SKILLS

Whoever finds the most eggs wins a/an _____ prize: a box
ADJECTIVE

full of _____! With a prize like this, you *have* to win. But
PLURAL NOUN

how? Follow these _____-proof tips, and you'll be a winner—
NOUN

or I'm a/an _____'s uncle!
NOUN

• Scout out the location of the egg hunt for every little nook and

_____ before it starts. Make a mental note of _____
NOUN   ADJECTIVE

hiding spots.

• Find a sturdy _____ to hold your eggs. The last thing you
NOUN

want is to lose because your basket _____ and you
VERB (PAST TENSE)

broke all your _____.
PLURAL NOUN

• Dress for success by wearing clothing that's easy to _____
VERB

in. For a look that's sure to intimidate the _____, put war
PLURAL NOUN

paint on your _____.
PART OF THE BODY

When the race begins and _____ says, "On your mark, get
PERSON IN ROOM

set, _____," you'll be two _____ ahead of the
VERB   PLURAL NOUN

competition!

MAD LIBS® is fun to play with friends, but you can also play it by yourself! To begin with, DO NOT look at the story on the page below. Fill in the blanks on this page with the words called for. Then, using the words you have selected, fill in the blank spaces in the story.

Now you've created your own hilarious MAD LIBS® game!

BUNNY CELEBS

NOUN _____

PLURAL NOUN _____

PART OF THE BODY (PLURAL) _____

NOUN _____

ADJECTIVE _____

PERSON IN ROOM _____

ADJECTIVE _____

A PLACE _____

ADJECTIVE _____

ADJECTIVE _____

NOUN _____

NOUN _____

VERB ENDING IN "ING" _____

SAME VERB ENDING IN "ING" _____

SAME VERB ENDING IN "ING" _____

PERSON IN ROOM _____

ADJECTIVE _____

PERSON IN ROOM _____

MAD LIBS

BUNNY CELEBS

The Easter Bunny may be the most famous _____ in all the
                                              NOUN
land, but these floppy-eared _____ have hopped their way
                                PLURAL NOUN
into people's hearts and _____, too.
                          PART OF THE BODY (PLURAL)

• **Bugs Bunny**—Known for his catchphrase "What's up, _____?"
                                                          NOUN

   Bugs Bunny is a cartoon rabbit with a/an _____ personality
                                              ADJECTIVE
   who loves to play tricks on _____. Bugs is so _____,
                                 PERSON IN ROOM   ADJECTIVE
   he even has a star on the _____ Walk of Fame!
                              A PLACE

• **The Energizer Bunny**—This _____ pink bunny is full of
                                  ADJECTIVE
   _____ energy—a good thing, considering he's the
        ADJECTIVE
   mascot for _____ batteries! As the commercials say, the
                 NOUN
   Energizer _____ "keeps _____ and
                NOUN   VERB ENDING IN "ING"
   _____ and _____!"
   SAME VERB ENDING IN "ING"   SAME VERB ENDING IN "ING"

• **Peter Rabbit**—Fictional Peter Rabbit became famous in Beatrix

   Potter's book *The Tale of* _____. He lives in a/an
                                PERSON IN ROOM
   _____ rabbit hole with his mother and his three sisters,
      ADJECTIVE
   Flopsy, Mopsy, and _____.
                       PERSON IN ROOM

From EASTER EGGSTRAVAGANZA MAD LIBS® • Copyright © 2013 by Penguin Random House LLC.

MAD LIBS® is fun to play with friends, but you can also play it by yourself! To begin with, DO NOT look at the story on the page below. Fill in the blanks on this page with the words called for. Then, using the words you have selected, fill in the blank spaces in the story.

Now you've created your own hilarious MAD LIBS® game!

CHOCOLATE THROUGH THE AGES

ADJECTIVE _____

ADJECTIVE _____

NUMBER _____

PLURAL NOUN _____

ADJECTIVE _____

TYPE OF LIQUID _____

ADJECTIVE _____

NOUN _____

PART OF THE BODY (PLURAL) _____

NOUN _____

TYPE OF LIQUID _____

ADJECTIVE _____

PART OF THE BODY _____

PLURAL NOUN _____

PLURAL NOUN _____

A PLACE _____

MAD LIBS®
CHOCOLATE THROUGH THE AGES

The history of chocolate, like the _____ treat itself, is rich
<u>ADJECTIVE</u>

and _____. In fact, you can trace its roots back _____
<u>ADJECTIVE</u>   <u>NUMBER</u>

years! Mayan and Aztec _____ in Central and South
<u>PLURAL NOUN</u>

America offered cacao seeds to their _____ gods and drank
<u>ADJECTIVE</u>

chocolate _____ during religious ceremonies. Back then,
<u>TYPE OF LIQUID</u>

chocolate tasted bitter and _____—nothing like the sweet
<u>ADJECTIVE</u>

_____ we know today. In the 1600s, chocolate became
<u>NOUN</u>

popular in Europe when King Louis XIII of France fell head over

_____ for this newfangled _____.
<u>PART OF THE BODY (PLURAL)</u>   <u>NOUN</u>

Europeans then added sugar and _____ to chocolate to
<u>TYPE OF LIQUID</u>

make it _____ and more pleasing to the _____ .
<u>ADJECTIVE</u>   <u>PART OF THE BODY</u>

In the late 1700s, the first United States factory to make chocolate

_____ opened. Since then, chocolate has been enjoyed by
<u>PLURAL NOUN</u>

_____ all over (the) _____!
<u>PLURAL NOUN</u>   <u>A PLACE</u>

MAD LIBS® is fun to play with friends, but you can also play it by yourself! To begin with, DO NOT look at the story on the page below. Fill in the blanks on this page with the words called for. Then, using the words you have selected, fill in the blank spaces in the story.

Now you've created your own hilarious MAD LIBS® game!

HOW TO DECORATE EASTER EGGS

ADJECTIVE _____

PLURAL NOUN _____

ADJECTIVE _____

NOUN _____

NOUN _____

NOUN _____

PART OF THE BODY _____

ADVERB _____

TYPE OF LIQUID _____

ADVERB _____

NOUN _____

TYPE OF LIQUID _____

NOUN _____

PART OF THE BODY (PLURAL) _____

NOUN _____

PLURAL NOUN _____

EXCLAMATION _____

ADJECTIVE _____

MAD☺LIBS®
HOW TO DECORATE
EASTER EGGS

Want to make the world's most _____ eggs that'll last and
ADJECTIVE
last for _____ to come? Just follow these _____
PLURAL NOUN   ADJECTIVE
instructions!

1. Poke two holes in the egg's _____ using a very pointy
NOUN
_____. Insert a small _____ into one of the
NOUN   NOUN
holes, place it to your _____, and blow _____.
PART OF THE BODY   ADVERB

2. Now that you have a hollow egg, rinse it with _____
TYPE OF LIQUID
and allow it to dry _____.
ADVERB

3. It's time to paint your _____! In separate containers, mix
NOUN
each tablet of color with a small amount of _____.
TYPE OF LIQUID
Use a/an _____ to hold the egg so you don't dye your
NOUN
_____, and dip the _____ into the dye.
PART OF THE BODY (PLURAL)   NOUN

4. Once the egg dries, you can decorate it with stickers, jewels, or
_____. _____! Now you have made a/an
PLURAL NOUN   EXCLAMATION
_____ Easter egg!
ADJECTIVE

MAD LIBS® is fun to play with friends, but you can also play it by yourself! To begin with, DO NOT look at the story on the page below. Fill in the blanks on this page with the words called for. Then, using the words you have selected, fill in the blank spaces in the story.

Now you've created your own hilarious MAD LIBS® game!

A HARE-Y SITUATION

NOUN _____

A PLACE _____

VERB (PAST TENSE) _____

ADVERB _____

NOUN _____

PART OF THE BODY _____

ADJECTIVE _____

NOUN _____

NOUN _____

PLURAL NOUN _____

ADVERB _____

NOUN _____

ADJECTIVE _____

ADVERB _____

NOUN _____

ADJECTIVE _____

PLURAL NOUN _____

NOUN _____

PART OF THE BODY (PLURAL) _____

NOUN _____

MAD LIBS®

A HARE-Y SITUATION

When I was a wee little _____, my parents took me to (the)
                          NOUN

_____ to see the Easter Bunny. I was so excited, I almost
   A PLACE

_____. We got in line, and I waited _____.
VERB (PAST TENSE)   ADVERB

When it was finally my turn, a/an _____ led me by the
                                          NOUN

_____ to see the Easter Bunny. But up close, he looked big
PART OF THE BODY

and _____. "Mommy, Mommy," I yelled, "I don't want to sit
       ADJECTIVE

on his _____! He's a scary _____!" But then I saw
         NOUN   NOUN

that the Easter Bunny had a basket full of candy _____.
                                                    PLURAL NOUN

He held it out to me, and I _____ walked toward him.
                                  ADVERB

"Here you go," he said, handing me a jelly _____. "It's okay.
                                               NOUN

Don't be _____." I sniffled and _____ took the
            ADJECTIVE   ADVERB

candy. He was a nice _____ after all, so I gave him a hug. His
                           NOUN

fur was soft and _____, and he smelled like _____.
                      ADJECTIVE   PLURAL NOUN

Just then, the flash of a/an _____ went off. To this day, I still
                                NOUN

have a picture of me, _____ red from crying,
                         PART OF THE BODY (PLURAL)

hugging the Easter _____!
                         NOUN

From EASTER EGGSTRAVAGANZA MAD LIBS® • Copyright © 2013 by Penguin Random House LLC.

MAD LIBS® is fun to play with friends, but you can also play it by yourself! To begin with, DO NOT look at the story on the page below. Fill in the blanks on this page with the words called for. Then, using the words you have selected, fill in the blank spaces in the story.

Now you've created your own hilarious MAD LIBS® game!

THE BEASTER BUNNY

NOUN _____

NUMBER _____

NOUN _____

NOUN _____

NUMBER _____

ADJECTIVE _____

NOUN _____

NUMBER _____

NOUN _____

NOUN _____

ADJECTIVE _____

A PLACE _____

PERSON IN ROOM _____

A PLACE _____

ADJECTIVE _____

NOUN _____

PERSON IN ROOM (FEMALE) _____

NOUN _____

MAD LIBS

THE BEASTER BUNNY

The world's largest _____ is a Continental Giant rabbit
 NOUN

named Darius. He weighs almost _____ pounds! He is four
 NUMBER

feet four inches long—that's the size of a small _____!
 NOUN

Darius is a very happy _____. He is three years old and
 NOUN

eats up to _____ carrots per day, in addition to two
 NUMBER

_____ meals of _____ mix, _____ apples,
 ADJECTIVE   NOUN   NUMBER

and an entire _____. He even eats his meals while sitting in
 NOUN

a/an _____ at the kitchen table! The _____ bunny gets
 NOUN   ADJECTIVE

plenty of exercise. He loves to run around (the) _____ all
 A PLACE

day. Darius lives with his owner, _____, in a small town in
 PERSON IN ROOM

(the) _____. His owner says that he has a/an _____
 A PLACE   ADJECTIVE

personality and that he thinks he's a/an _____! Darius's
 NOUN

mother, _____, held the record of world's
 PERSON IN ROOM (FEMALE)

largest rabbit prior to Darius. Guess the apple doesn't fall far from

the _____!
 NOUN

MAD LIBS® is fun to play with friends, but you can also play it by yourself! To begin with, DO NOT look at the story on the page below. Fill in the blanks on this page with the words called for. Then, using the words you have selected, fill in the blank spaces in the story.

Now you've created your own hilarious MAD LIBS® game!

A RECIPE FOR MARSHMALLOWS

ADJECTIVE _____

NOUN _____

ADJECTIVE _____

TYPE OF LIQUID _____

NOUN _____

TYPE OF LIQUID _____

ADJECTIVE _____

NOUN _____

ADJECTIVE _____

ADJECTIVE _____

NUMBER _____

TYPE OF LIQUID _____

VERB _____

ADJECTIVE _____

NOUN _____

NOUN _____

EXCLAMATION _____

PLURAL NOUN _____

NUMBER _____

MAD LIBS®
A RECIPE FOR MARSHMALLOWS

Store-bought marshmallows are a/an _____ Easter treat—
_____ ADJECTIVE

but you can make even better ones in the comfort of your own

_____. Just follow these _____ instructions:
NOUN   ADJECTIVE

Pour gelatin and a half cup of _____ into a large
                               TYPE OF LIQUID

_____. Next, put a half cup of _____, two cups
NOUN   TYPE OF LIQUID

of _____ sugar, and a cup of _____ syrup into
   ADJECTIVE   NOUN

a/an _____ saucepan over _____ heat. Once the
     ADJECTIVE   ADJECTIVE

mixture reaches _____ degrees Fahrenheit, add a dash of
                NUMBER

_____. Remove the pan from heat and combine its
TYPE OF LIQUID

contents with the gelatin water. Briskly _____ the mixture
                                         VERB

until it becomes foamy and _____, then pour it into a/an
                           ADJECTIVE

_____-coated _____ to cool. _____!
NOUN   NOUN   EXCLAMATION

You have your very own homemade _____. It's as easy as
                                PLURAL NOUN

one, two, _____.
          NUMBER

MAD LIBS® is fun to play with friends, but you can also play it by yourself! To begin with, DO NOT look at the story on the page below. Fill in the blanks on this page with the words called for. Then, using the words you have selected, fill in the blank spaces in the story.

Now you've created your own hilarious MAD LIBS® game!

AN EASTER MENU

ADJECTIVE _____

PERSON IN ROOM _____

ADJECTIVE _____

PLURAL NOUN _____

PLURAL NOUN _____

PLURAL NOUN _____

NOUN _____

ADJECTIVE _____

PLURAL NOUN _____

NOUN _____

PLURAL NOUN _____

PLURAL NOUN _____

NOUN _____

NOUN _____

NOUN _____

NOUN _____

PART OF THE BODY _____

VERB _____

MAD LIBS®

AN EASTER MENU

What's that _____ smell? Why, it's a delicious Easter meal,
    ADJECTIVE

cooked by _____! Here's the _____ menu:
  PERSON IN ROOM   ADJECTIVE

Appetizer: deviled eggs sprinkled with paprika and _____
               PLURAL NOUN

Salad: tomatoes and roast _____ on a bed of tender
         PLURAL NOUN

baby _____
  PLURAL NOUN

Main Dish: a/an _____ -baked _____-cut ham
       NOUN   ADJECTIVE

glazed with _____ and sweet _____ juice
    PLURAL NOUN   NOUN

Sides: mashed _____, braised _____, and
      PLURAL NOUN   PLURAL NOUN

_____-bread pudding
 NOUN

Dessert: coconut _____ pie à la _____ with whipped
      NOUN   NOUN

_____ on top
 NOUN

Is your _____ watering yet? I hope so, because it's time to
  PART OF THE BODY

_____!
 VERB

MAD LIBS® is fun to play with friends, but you can also play it by yourself! To begin with, DO NOT look at the story on the page below. Fill in the blanks on this page with the words called for. Then, using the words you have selected, fill in the blank spaces in the story.

Now you've created your own hilarious MAD LIBS® game!

RABBITS RUN AMOK

NUMBER _____

ADJECTIVE _____

NOUN _____

NOUN _____

PLURAL NOUN _____

NOUN _____

ADJECTIVE _____

PLURAL NOUN _____

PLURAL NOUN _____

PLURAL NOUN _____

PART OF THE BODY (PLURAL) _____

ADJECTIVE _____

NOUN _____

A PLACE _____

VERB _____

ADJECTIVE _____

RABBITS RUN AMOK

Did you know there are more than _____ rabbit breeds? It's
_____NUMBER_____
true! Here's a list of some of the most _____ kinds of bunnies.
_____ADJECTIVE_____

- **The Lop**—This floppy-eared _____ is the fanciest
  _____NOUN_____
  _____ of all. Lops were bred in England as pets for
  _____NOUN_____
  _____, and are the oldest domestic _____.
  __PLURAL NOUN__   NOUN

- **The Angora**—The Angora rabbit comes from Turkey and was bred
  for its long, _____ fur, which is sheared and used to knit
  _____ADJECTIVE_____
  soft, cozy _____.
  __PLURAL NOUN__

- **The Netherland Dwarf**—Weighing less than two _____,
  _____PLURAL NOUN_____
  the Netherland Dwarf is one of the smallest _____. They
  _____PLURAL NOUN_____
  are beloved for their babylike _____ and their
  _____PART OF THE BODY (PLURAL)_____
  _____ demeanor.
  __ADJECTIVE__

And finally, did you know that the hare isn't even a type of
_____ at all? Instead of living in burrows like rabbits, they
__NOUN__
live in nests in (the) _____. And they _____ alone
_____A PLACE_____   VERB
instead of in groups! You learn something _____ every day.
_____ADJECTIVE_____

MAD LIBS® is fun to play with friends, but you can also play it by yourself! To begin with, DO NOT look at the story on the page below. Fill in the blanks on this page with the words called for. Then, using the words you have selected, fill in the blank spaces in the story.

Now you've created your own hilarious MAD LIBS® game!

THE EASTER BUNNY AND SANTA CLAUS: BFFS, PART 1

PLURAL NOUN _____

ADJECTIVE _____

VERB ENDING IN "ING" _____

ADJECTIVE _____

A PLACE _____

PLURAL NOUN _____

NOUN _____

PLURAL NOUN _____

NOUN _____

PLURAL NOUN _____

PLURAL NOUN _____

ADJECTIVE _____

NOUN _____

THE EASTER BUNNY AND SANTA CLAUS: BFFS, PART 1

What, you didn't know the Easter Bunny and Santa are best

_____ forever? It's true! To prove it, here's a/an _____
  PLURAL NOUN   ADJECTIVE

e-mail from the Easter Bunny to Santa:

Hey, Santa, how's it _____? Everything's _____
                              VERB ENDING IN "ING"   ADJECTIVE

in my little burrow here in (the) _____. I'm just gearing up
                                   A PLACE

for another Easter: painting and decorating _____, growing
                                        PLURAL NOUN

plastic grass in my _____, filling plastic eggs with
                              NOUN

_____—you know, the usual. But I can't wait for Easter
  PLURAL NOUN

Sunday! How can you stand to wait a whole _____ in
                                         NOUN

between delivering _____ to good little girls and
                            PLURAL NOUN

_____? Let me know if you have any _____ tips.
  PLURAL NOUN   ADJECTIVE

Your _____ forever,
          NOUN

The Easter Bunny

MAD LIBS® is fun to play with friends, but you can also play it by yourself! To begin with, DO NOT look at the story on the page below. Fill in the blanks on this page with the words called for. Then, using the words you have selected, fill in the blank spaces in the story.

Now you've created your own hilarious MAD LIBS® game!

THE EASTER BUNNY AND SANTA CLAUS: BFFS, PART 2

ADJECTIVE _____

NOUN _____

ADJECTIVE _____

PLURAL NOUN _____

PLURAL NOUN _____

PLURAL NOUN _____

PART OF THE BODY (PLURAL) _____

NOUN _____

VERB ENDING IN "ING" _____

NOUN _____

PLURAL NOUN _____

ADJECTIVE _____

VERB ENDING IN "ING" _____

NOUN _____

Need more proof? Here's Santa's _____ response!
                                    ADJECTIVE

Dear E. Bunny,

Ho, ho, ho, my furry little _____! Things in the North Pole
                                NOUN

are as _____ as ever. Believe it or not, the elves are already
          ADJECTIVE

making _____ for next Christmas! And Mrs. Claus is getting a
          PLURAL NOUN

head start on baking Christmas _____. I agree, it is tough
                                    PLURAL NOUN

waiting to deliver _____ to children everywhere. All I want
                      PLURAL NOUN

is to put smiles on their _____. My suggestion
                              PART OF THE BODY (PLURAL)

would be to pick up a hobby, like _____ riding or putt-putt
                                      NOUN

_____. Myself, I go _____ fishing or I knit
VERB ENDING IN "ING"   NOUN

_____—Mrs. Claus taught me how! (I think she was tired of
PLURAL NOUN

darning my _____ socks for me! Ho, ho, ho!) Before you
              ADJECTIVE

know it, Easter will be _____ on your front door!
                          VERB ENDING IN "ING"

With all my _____,
              NOUN

Santa

Download Mad Libs today!

Join the millions of Mad Libs fans
creating wacky and wonderful
stories on our apps!